Sally and the STEM Com-petition

The Number Investigators 3

Martin Tiller

ISBN: 978-0-9996879-3-2

For Rachel

Thanks to Jenifer Ring for her help with the book and her continued support.

To all students who enjoy numbers and enjoy math.

Table of Contents

Chapter 1 Sally Hemingway

My name is Sally Hemingway, and I am the only girl in my family. I have a big family. I have three brothers. First, there's Michael who is in the fifth grade. I am the second oldest in the family, and I am in the third grade. Next is Jackson, who is in Kindergarten. And Austin is eight months old. He is still in diapers and makes a lot of noise. But he is cute. Other than my mother, as I said I am the only girl, but she's an adult. And then there's Dad.

I am in the third grade at Turing Elementary School. Mrs. King is my teacher. She's been teaching there like forever, longer than I have been alive.

Charlotte is my best friend. We are in a club we call The Number Investigators. We started the group in the first grade. That year our first-grade teacher, Mrs. Whitlow, would say "Let's investigate numbers!" when it was time for math. That got me and Charlotte into math. We used to run around the playground shouting, "Let's investigate numbers!" We would count the number of monkey bars, or the number of people on the kickball field, or the number of rocks we found. After a while, we pretty much counted everything on the playground. So, we started our own club to spend more time thinking and talking about numbers. We had two others join us as well in the group, Marcus Jones joined us in the second grade when he moved into the neighborhood and then he proceeded to beat

Charlotte in the second-grade math bee. When he did that, we let him in the club.

Aaron Chu joined the club in second grade as well. We let him join when we saw him bring a chessboard to school and he counted the number of pawns in the box. We didn't know how to play chess, but we liked that he counted, and chess seems to have something to do with numbers. He also plays a lot of sports and memorizes the stats on the back of baseball cards.

So, it's a very cool club. And we do a lot of things together.

This week our teacher, Mrs. King, told us that Turing Elementary School is having a STEM competition. What's a STEM competition? STEM means: Science, Technology, Engineering, Math.

In the competition, teams have to use at least two of the four things to solve or create something the instructor tells them to make.

I admit when Charlotte and I started the Number Investigators, I did it mostly for the fun. I didn't care much about the numbers. I did it for hanging out with my best friend. But the more we did it, the more I liked working with numbers. And not only that, I liked all the things we made. From playing with Marcus' Magnix set, to the set-up for Charlotte's Lemonade stand. I have learned to like making things using numbers and science. Participating in the Math

Bee was fun, but it was only numbers. I want to make something, and that's why I want to do the STEM competition.

No, change that. I don't want to do the STEM competition.

I want to win it.

Chapter 2 The STEM Competition

To back up a little, this is how my pursuit of winning the STEM competition began.

"Okay, class I want you to get out your science binders," said Mrs. King. "We are going to review our simple machines test."

The class let out a groan. Charlotte and I looked at each other and smiled, we knew we probably did really well.

Simple machines are things that help us do work, things like an inclined plane, wheel and axle, pulley, lever, wedge, and screw.

Mrs. King walked by my desk and placed my test face down on my desk. "Nicely done, Sally," she said as she kept walking and passing out tests.

I turned the paper over – a hundred percent. "Yes!" I pumped my fist into the air.

Charlotte did the same. She smiled and showed her test with the big 100 written in green across the top.

"A 55!" shouted Gavin Eggleston from a few feet away.

"Thank you, Gavin, keep your voice down please,"

Mrs. King didn't even look at him she just kept walking.

Mrs. King stood at the front of the class. "Okay, we don't have time to review the whole test, but question three was missed the most, so let's take a look at it." Mrs. King had the test up on the screen at the front of the room. The question was about a door stop, "A lot of us put down that a door stop is an inclined plane."

"It is! I used one at my house as a ramp with my cars," shouted Gavin.

"Use your inside voice Gavin, or you can stand with me during recess," Mrs. King replied. "But yes, Gavin it does look like an incline plane. But in the photograph, how are they using the door stop? Are they using it as a ramp? Are there cars jumping off the door stop?"

"No," Gavin replied quietly. He sank into his seat and threw his pencil down on his desk.

"They are using the doorstop as they are supposed to use it. They are wedging it underneath the door, thus keeping the door from moving. Understand?"

Gavin nodded his head, and several other people said "Yes," as they flipped through the test.

Mrs. King went over several other questions and began to wrap it up, "So those were the most missed questions. Are there any other questions out there that I didn't go over?"

No one spoke. We hate reviewing tests. I mean we've already taken a test, which is bad enough, and now we have to go through the experience again? Umm...Thanks, but no. Even if I did get a 100%, thank you very much!

"Okay, so take your tests home. Your parents will be expecting them, I emailed your parents and informed them they would be going home today. But we're not quite done with simple machines." The picture on the Smartboard changed. The words STEM Competition appeared at the top of the screen in large blue letters.

"The school is hosting a STEM competition in three weeks. There will be teams from each grade 3-5, as well as teams from Holly Hills and Cedarwood Road Elementary Schools. Teams will consist of four people. So, think about joining. It sounds like it will be fun. Mrs. Russell from Kindergarten will be leading our school's teams."

Charlotte and I looked at each other and smiled.

"We should enter this!" she whispered to me.

"Of course we should, and we should win it!" I whispered back.

We had a new item for the Number Investigators meeting.

Chapter 3 Treehouse Meeting

"Hear ye! Hear ye! This meeting of the Number Investigators can now come to order!" Charlotte pounded the floor of the treehouse with her gavel, as she called the group meeting to order, a gavel is a fancy looking hammer that judges use to get people's attention in a courtroom.

"You should have never been given that gavel," Marcus shook his head and covered his ears.

"I like my gavel," said Charlotte.

"We know!" replied Marcus.

"Who has brought their math homework?" Charlotte asked.

"We all did. Let's skip ahead in the agenda, and talk about the STEM competition," I said. I held up the STEM competition flier. Charlotte would take forever to go through her regular agenda in a meeting – math homework, things we brought to count. It's always the same, and I didn't have the patience for being the same tonight.

"What about it?" Marcus asked.

"Are we going to do it?" I asked.

"I hadn't thought about it. It's on a Saturday. I probably have a baseball game," Aaron said.

"I hadn't thought of that," I said. My heart sank, I was counting on all of us being able to participate.

"When is it? What's the date?" Charlotte asked. She sensed my disappointment.

I held up the flier from school. "April 24th, and it begins at 9:30 AM," I said.

"I definitely have a baseball game," Aaron said.

"What were to happen if you were to skip the game?" Charlotte asked.

Aaron made a face, "My coach and my parents would kill me, not to mention my teammates. I need to be there."

"Marcus? Can you make it?" I asked.

"I think so, I will have to double check with my parents though," he replied.

"Do you want to do it Marcus?" I asked.

"Sure, it could be fun to make things and to see if we win. Especially since we all couldn't win the school Math Bee."

"None of us won the school Math Bee, remember Sanjey won it," Charlotte reminded him.

"Of course, I remember!" Marcus shouted. "But only one of us could win the Math Bee, and you were the third-grade winner. All of us together could win this." He made a circle with his index finger, pointing at all of us in the treehouse.

"Now don't go trying to make me feel guilty now," Aaron replied.

Charlotte banged her gavel. "Okay, let's move on. The three of us will participate in the STEM contest, at least once we check with our parents." Charlotte nodded her head at Marcus.

"No!" I replied. The other three raised their eyebrows and looked at me. "I mean, the contest is supposed to have four people. Who is going to be the fourth person? If Aaron can't do it, then who can?"

The treehouse was silent for a moment as everyone looked at floor and thought.

"How about Gavin?" Charlotte offered.

"Gavin? Really?" I replied. "He hates math, and I am sure he wouldn't want to spend his Saturday at school."

"What about Sanjey? Since he won the math bee," Aaron asked.

"He's a fifth grader. It needs to be another third grader," I replied.

"Well, I don't know who else to ask right now," said Charlotte. "We can ask people at school tomorrow, to see if anyone else wants to be on our team."

"Okay, I guess that's what we'll have to do," I replied.

"Now who brought items to count or play with?" Charlotte shouted.

Marcus brought out his Magnix set and we played with that for the afternoon, building things together.

But I was down one for the STEM competition, it looked like we would not all be building together on that project.

Being one man down made it harder to win.

Chapter 4 Hamburgers

I walked home from Charlotte's after we played with Marcus's Magnix set. There was still light outside. Jackson, my five-year-old brother who was in Kindergarten was running around the backyard with a water gun, shooting Michael my oldest brother, who was in the fifth grade.

"Sally do you want to play?" asked Jackson. He pointed his green water gun at me and pulled the trigger. The water hit me in stomach, soaking my shirt. "Here's a gun!" He threw a purple water gun at me.

"No, I don't want to get wet!" and I threw the gun right back him. He ducked to keep the gun from hitting him in his forehead.

"I think she's going to kill you later!" said Michael.

"Her shirt is just wet, it will dry," was the last thing I heard Jackson say as I walked in the back door to the kitchen.

I went into the kitchen counter, grabbed a paper towel and tried to dry my shirt off.

"Did the boys get you?" Dad asked. He was cooking hamburgers for supper.

"Yes, it was Jackson," I replied wiping my shirt.

"Do you want me to ground them? Ground them

both until they are 21? They can't go outside, they can only go to school?" he said.

I rolled my eyes. "Dad! You know someday, I am going to call you on that, and you're going to have to keep them in the house forever." He always threatens to ground my brothers until they are 21. As annoying as my brothers are, I think locking them away into the house would be a terrible idea. I don't want them in the house all the time. I need them to be outside and away from me, maybe he can build a cage for them and leave them in there.

"Well, just let me know. I am fully prepared."

"Okay, Dad!" I waved at him and went to my room.

Normally, I would be out there giving Jackson and Michael a run for their money with the water guns. But I was thinking about the STEM competition. What sort of tasks would they give us? How good would the competition be? I tried not to be sad about Aaron not wanting to be in the competition with me. He was good at sports. But he was also good at math, and this STEM competition would be right up his alley.

I looked at the flier that came from the school. There was a picture of students building a structure with just toothpicks and marshmallows. An idea popped into my head.

I pulled out a package of toothpicks. The toothpicks were left over from a science project I did in January. I had made different ocean animals; fish, whales, octopus, out of play dough, and I put them in front of a backdrop of the ocean.

The box was still nearly full of toothpicks.

I didn't have any marshmallows, but I did have a ton of bubble gum. I like bubble gum and chewing gum. I like collecting bubble gum. I am a connoisseur of gum. But for this project I would just use the plainest and cheapest gum I had, so I pulled some from my stash of Rick's Mint chewing gum that was hidden under my desk. I started chewing.

Using only a small piece of gum, and not the whole piece, I attached a piece of chewing gum to the ends of the toothpicks and I began to build. And as I ran out of gum, I began a new piece. After a few minutes, there was a tower about a foot tall on my desk.

There was another difference between my tower and the one in the picture, other than the fact I used chewing gum instead of marshmallows, I put crossbeams that made Xs between the different legs of the tower. This step was always missed when people would build things with marshmallows and toothpicks. They just use the legs to try and make the structure as tall as they can, without giving it the needed support.

There was a knock on the door, it was Mom. "Sally,

come on down, it's dinner time." She tilted her head, "What's that?" She pointed at my chewing gum and toothpick tower.

"A tower," I replied.

"I can see that. Any particular reason for a tower with bubble gum as the glue?" she replied.

I showed her the flier to STEM competition, "I was practicing for this."

Mom took the flier in her hand and read it over. "This looks interesting," she replied. "You want to go to this?"

I nodded my head, "Yes. I want to go."

"Tell us about it during diner. Dad made hamburgers for us."

Mom and I walked downstairs. All the boys in the house were already sitting down at the table. Austin sat in a highchair. His bib was placed around his neck. A smiling elephant juggling a blue ball was on the bib. The elephant would be covered in food by the end of dinner.

I sat down next to Michael. Mom sat down next to Austin.

"Honey, Sally wants to go to a STEM competition at school," Mom said before anyone else could say anything.

Michael turned and looked at me, "You want to go the STEM competition at school? On a Saturday?"

Mom shot him a look. "Michael, if your sister wants to go, that is very cool of her. Don't put her down for wanting to do something at school."

"What's a STEM competition? Does that have something to do with flowers or trees?" Jackson asked with his mouth full of hamburger.

"Close your mouth. That's gross," I said. "STEM stands for Science-Technology-Engineering-Math."

Jackson swallowed. "Engineering as in driving trains?" Jackson's face lit up like a Christmas tree.

"No. Engineering as in making and designing things so they work properly," I replied.

"And technology as in like computers and phones?" Jackson spoke fast.

"Yes, technology as in computers and phones, but in other things as well, like electricity or machines," I said.

"I want to do that," Jackson looked at Mom then at me.

"Sorry buddy. No teams for Kindergartners. When you're older and in the third grade," I told him.

"Oh, man! Why is it I always have to be older!" he

shouted.

"Jackson, stop yelling at the table," Dad instructed him.

Dad passed the potato chips down the table, "So, how does this competition work? Do you work by yourself? Does Mrs. King assign you your team?"

"I'm trying to get The Number Investigators go with me," I said.

"What do you mean...trying?" Mom asked.

"I don't know if Aaron will be able to go. He says he has a baseball game that day," I said. She sensed my disappointment.

"Well, a lot of sports are played on the weekend. And if his team already had that day scheduled, he should go to that," Mom said.

"I know, but I think Charlotte is definitely going. And Marcus is checking with his parents tonight," I said.

Mom smiled at me, "Well, that's good."

"But I need four people. So, I am still stuck." I replied.

Austin then spit up a ton of carrots, and they tumbled all down his bib. I swear I don't know how such little things can hold so much food.

“Ewww!” Jackson shouted.

“Jackson, stop yelling at the dinner table,” said Dad as he bit into a hamburger.

And with the great erupting Austin taking Mom’s attention, we didn’t talk anymore about the STEM competition for the rest of dinner.

Chapter 5 Forming Groups

At the start of science class, Mrs. King put the STEM flier on the Smartboard and pointed to it. "I gave you information about the STEM competition yesterday. Has anyone decided to try the competition or to make a team? I can always put together groups if people don't have a complete group."

My stomach sank. That would be a great risk if Mrs. King was in charge of assigning us a fourth group member. Charlotte looked at me and then didn't say anything.

"Anyone?" Mrs. King asked the class again.

Charlotte looked back at me and mouthed "Say something!"

"Charlotte, is there something you would like to share with the class?" Mrs. King asked. Charlotte's face went red.

I raised my hand to help my friend. "Mrs. King, I want to be in the competition. Me and Charlotte, and I think Marcus, are going to go as a group."

"That's only three. Do you need me to find you another person?"

"Mrs. King, if we can't find another person, or if you can't find another person, would we still be able to participate? Would it have to be four people? I mean if there are two other groups of four from the third grade, and just the remaining three of us. Well, I don't think that would be fair for us not to be able to participate simply because there isn't four people exactly in our group."

The class was silent.

I realized my mistake. I had never challenged a teacher like that before. I mean others had, but not me.

"Sally, you make a valid point. Mrs. Russell in Kindergarten is the teacher in charge. I will ask her what she thinks about your question." She looked around the room. "Is there anyone else that wants to participate in the STEM competition?" Mrs. King looked around the room, her finger pointing as she looked.

"Yes, we want to participate," said Juan Ramos. He wore a Star Wars shirt and khaki shorts.

"Good, Juan. Who is we?" Mrs. King asked.

"Me and Kadan," Juan motioned across the room to Kadan Lawrence.

"Do you have anyone else that you want to be a part of your team?" Mrs. King asked.

Juan shook his head.

"I might be able to find two other people, maybe someone from Mrs. Wilson's class. We just decided to do this yesterday," Kadan said.

Mrs. King smiled, "I will check with Mrs. Wilson or Mrs. Buchanan to see if there is anyone else that can fill-in for your two groups. Maybe they have the right numbers. Okay, let's move on, and begin our science lesson. Get out your science binder," said Mrs. King as she turned to the Smartboard.

Chapter 6 We Should Have Thought of Him

"I should have thought of asking Kadan!" I said as I sat down at the lunch table.

"Why Kadan?" Charlotte asked as she opened her milk.

"His dad is an engineer. He designs airplane parts. He would be a natural at the STEM competition," I explained.

Marcus sat down across from me and put his tray down, "Yeah, Kadan always does well in science. We should have thought of him last night."

"What are we talking about?" Aaron asked as he sat down next to Marcus.

"We should have thought of asking Kadan to join us," I said.

"Oh, still talking about the STEM competition," Aaron looked disappointed.

"Sorry, but yes we are," I replied.

"Why are you guys talking about me?" Kadan leaned over the lunch table from several seats away.

The four of us looked at each other embarrassed.

"We need one more person for our group, and we didn't think about asking you. You're good in science," I said.

"Thanks! But Juan asked me yesterday. It will be fun to compete." He was being nice. I didn't feel like being nice. I wanted to win. And right now, I wasn't even sure we were going to get to be in the competition.

Chapter 7 The ER

After we got off the bus, Jackson and Michael ran home. I came in behind them. They bolted up the stairs in front of me.

I went into my bedroom and threw my backpack onto my bed.

"Sally come and shoot water guns with us!" Jackson shouted from his bedroom.

"Stop running in the house," Mom shouted from the living room.

"I bet you can't get me," he shouted. I felt a cold sensation on my back. I spun around and saw that little booger with a water gun pointed right at me. His eyes were bright and wide open, his massive grin showed his teeth. He was so happy.

And he was so dead.

"I am going to get you!" And I darted after him. He screamed as he bounded down the stairs.

"Stop running in the house!" Mom shouted once more from the living room.

Jackson sprinted into the kitchen, nearly tripping as he caught himself with his left hand, and he blasted out the back door, screaming with glee the whole way. I was in full pursuit. He made his way across the back deck in two steps. He jumped from the top of the stairs and landed on both feet on the paved walkway. He jumped right up and ran up the backyard hill. He was still screaming at the top of his lungs.

I did not have a water gun to shoot him with. It was my plan to grab him and take one from him. He sprinted up the hill. I grabbed his right arm and pulled it towards me. He fell. I landed on top of him, and I tumbled over him. I landed on my back looking up at the blue sky.

That's when I heard the screaming.

And boy was it loud.

"Owww!!! It hurts! It hurts!" he screamed.

I jumped up. Jackson's face was covered in tears and his face was beet red.

And his arm was crooked.

"What's wrong!" shouted Mom as she bolted out the back door.

"We fell down chasing each other," I stammered. Tears started to come out of my eyes.

"His arm is broken, Sally!" Mom pointed to the obvious injury.

I began to cry.

"We have to get him to the hospital," Mom said. "Go get in the car now!"

I stood still for second wondering if Mom was going to need help with Jackson.

"Get to the car now, Sally!"

Michael came out the back door, "What's going on?"

"Jackson's arm is broken, go inside, get Austin and put him in the car. I am going to get Jackson into the car, and we are all going to the ER. Go and do what I told you, now." She picked Jackson up and held him as if was still a baby, and she walked quickly to car. Jackson continued to scream a blood curdling scream. It made my stomach hurt and my heart ache for the little guy.

Michael got Austin into the car and we were off to the hospital. Mom called Dad at work as we headed to the ER.

Jackson continued to scream the whole way. His face damp from tears. The top of his shirt wet.

Austin for once didn't make a sound. He looked around with a concerned look on his face. He seemed to know something was wrong and now was not the time to be adding to the noise.

I cried, too.

I cried because I felt really sorry for my brother.

And because I knew I was going to die.

We got to the hospital and because Jackson was still screaming bloody murder the nurses came to him right away.

I sat in the waiting room with Michael and Austin. Austin still furrowed his brow as he looked around the room, he knew something was up. Dad came in and came over to us.

"So, what happened?" he asked clearly concerned.

I started crying again. "I was chasing him in the backyard, I grabbed his arm, and we fell on top of each other..." I couldn't finish the sentence as I cried.

Dad let out a deep breath and hugged me. "It's okay, Sally. It was an accident." He held me for a little more. "Okay, I need to go find him and your mother. Are you okay keeping Austin with you?"

"Austin is fine. Go check on Jackson," said Michael.

The nurses led Dad to the back.

An hour later, after walking Austin up and down the waiting room, Jackson came out with Mom and Dad. His right arm was in a cast from his wrist to his elbow and held in a blue sling.

Jackson wasn't crying anymore. His face was clean. The top of his shirt was still stained from the tears.

"How are you buddy?" asked Michael.

"I got a cast!" He held it up with pride. "I can't wait to have everyone at school sign it."

"So, you're feeling better then?" Michael replied.

"They gave him some good pain medicine," Mom informed us.

"I am glad to see that you are doing okay. I am sorry this happened." I put my arm around him.

"It's okay. It didn't hurt much," Jackson said.

And we all burst out laughing.

Chapter 8 Pizza

After the hospital we went to Giovanni's restaurant for some take-out pizza. We don't normally have pizza in the middle of the week. It's normally a Friday or a Saturday meal. But neither Mom nor Dad felt like making supper after everything that happened for the day. This was an out of the ordinary Thursday night. And Jackson likes the cheese pizza from Giovanni's. We came home with a cheese pizza and a pepperoni pizza.

Since Jackson was right-handed, he was eager to learn how to eat with just his left hand. Which is good, most of the people I know that broke their arms with their main arm complained. Jackson was eager to become ambidextrous, which means the ability to use both arms equally.

He learned the new word at the hospital from the doctor who put on the cast.

I was thankful that he was excited about trying to become ambidextrous. Because It's not like he was learning how to write his letters or anything important like that in Kindergarten.

We sat around the table and Mom sat next to Jackson. She mothered him, by feeding him his pizza.

"Mom! I can eat! Let me try with my left hand! I want to be ambidextrous!" he shouted.

"I get the feeling we are going to hear that word a lot over the next month or so," Michael said.

"I just don't want you getting it on your cast," Mom replied.

"He's going to get his cast dirty, might as well get used to it now," Dad replied. "I don't think you're going to go to school and feed him there are you?"

Mom made a face at Dad, "Maybe I will." And she stuck her tongue out at him.

"Mom! I don't want you coming to school to feed me! I want to learn how to eat with my left hand! I want to be ambidextrous!" Jackson shouted again.

"Okay, fine. Just don't get it on your clothes." Mom put the piece of pizza down on Jackson's plate and went back to eating her slice of pepperoni.

Jackson picked up his pizza with his left hand.

And then he dropped it on his shirt.

"Uh! Oh! Dang it!" he shouted.

Michael giggled.

Austin squealed.

"Ugh! I knew it!" my mom shouted as she got up and grabbed a paper towel to wipe off his shirt. She scrubbed his shirt with the paper towel.

"Mom!" Jackson shouted.

"Just let her clean it, and then we can try again," said Dad pulling on Jackson's shirt to help keep it straight for Mom.

Mom finished cleaning, and Jackson reached across the plate and grabbed another piece with his left hand. Dad picked up the plate to get it closer to Jackson. This time he was successful in get the pizza of the plate and onto his plate, keeping the plate in place with his cast. Once his plate was set, he picked up the pizza with his left hand, took a bite, and put it back onto the plate without dropping it or making a mess. He threw his left hand into the air, and lifted his cast a few inches off the table, "Yes! I am officially ambidextrous!"

Dad laughed, "Good job with the pizza! But... um...you're not quite ambidextrous yet!"

"Why not?" Jackson asked.

"I would say when you can write, and throw with your left hand as well as you can with your right hand, then you are ambidextrous. That's what the word means," Dad patted Jackson on the shoulder.

"Well, let me keep trying." Jackson picked up his pizza again and ate two more pieces without making a mess. He seemed to be enjoying this.

Mom relaxed a little, "Good job, honey."

We finished eating both pizzas.

"Okay, Jackson you can be dismissed," Mom instructed. He jumped down from the table. "Michael, go watch him." Michael cleaned up his plate and followed Jackson into the living room.

My stomach sank. I had not been dismissed from the table yet.

"Okay, let's talk," Mom put both her elbows on the table and raised her eyebrows. That was the look of death. "What happened today? I only got that you were chasing him."

"He started it," I spit the words out without thinking.

"Sally Hemingway! Try again," Mom replied. Dad sat with his arms crossed staring at me.

"He shot me with a water gun in my room. He got my back all soaked. I then chased him outside."

"That's why you two were sprinting in the house," Mom looked at Dad.

Dad raised his eyebrows. "Go on..."

"Then he ran out the door into the yard. And we fell on top of each other," I said.

Mom tilted her head at me, "How did his arm break? It didn't break because you tumbled on top of him."

I took a deep breath, well aware that it could very well be my last one, "I reached for the water gun in his right hand, and that's when he tripped or when we fell."

Dad leaned forward and put his arms on the table, "So you grabbed his right arm it sounds like, and that's when you two fell."

Tears dripped down my cheeks, "Yes, I think that's what happened."

We sat in silence. Austin kicked in his seat.

"I think you were a little rougher than you intended to be," Mom said finally. "I think there needs to be some sort of consequence." Mom looked at dad. She was fishing for punishment ideas.

"Maybe there shouldn't be any STEM competition." The words came like a kick to the stomach out of Dad's mouth.

"No!" I replied.

Mom took a deep breath, "Well, there needs to be some sort of consequence. Yes, it was an accident. But you were involved in breaking your brother's arm." Mom looked at Dad. "Since the STEM competition is a part of school, you can still go to that. I would say you can't have friends over or go over to friends house for the next week."

I accepted my fate, "Okay."

No Number Investigator Meetings for a week.

Chapter 9 The Most Popular Kindergartener

Jackson loved showing off his cast at school. He was the most popular Kindergartner that day. It seemed like teachers would stare at me if they saw me in the hallway. The whole school knew that Jackson Hemingway had broken his arm, and it was his sister Sally's fault.

Yay me.

"So, what happened again with your brother?" Charlotte asked me as we did our lap around the track at the start of recess.

"I was chasing him, and I grabbed his arm and fell on top of him. That's how he broke his arm."

"Oh."

"It also means no Number Investigator meetings for the next week. And you can't come over for just fun either," I looked at my feet. I was embarrassed.

"I figured you were going to say something like that. Remember, my parents grounded me because Charlie ate my mom's shoes."

I laughed, "Yeah."

"Parents do that sort of thing," Charlotte said trying to make me feel better.

Marcus and Aaron came running up behind us. "Okay, what happened again with your brother?" Marcus asked.

"I was chasing him, and I feel on top of him. That's how I broke his arm.

"Ouch," Marcus replied. "Did he cry?"

"Oh, did he ever cry! He cried so much it made me cry. He just screamed the whole way to the ER."

"Poor little guy," Aaron said. "How long is he going to be in the cast?"

"Six weeks, I think. He's hoping to become ambidextrous by the time they take the cast off."

Marcus and Aaron laughed.

"I remember breaking my arm in the first grade, I had to learn how to write with my left hand," said Marcus.

"Oh, then he'll love to hear how you did that."

"I complained the whole time, and did my best to not write," Marcus smiled at the memory.

"Are we meeting this afternoon at the treehouse?" Aaron asked.

"I guess so," Charlotte replied.

“I can’t go,” I replied. “I can’t go over to Charlotte’s house, and you guys can’t come over for a week,” I told the boys.

“Because of your brother?” Marcus asked.

“Yeah, my parents are mad at me for breaking his arm.”

“Oh!” Marcus replied. “That stinks!”

Gavin ran up behind us. “Hey! What happened with your brother? How did he break his arm?”

“Ugh!” I shouted.

“What?” Gavin shrugged his shoulders in defense.

Charlotte rescued me, “Sally accidentally fell down on him while they were running.”

“Oh, um, sorry to hear,” Gavin sensed my frustration.

“Sorry Gavin, everyone just keeps asking me about it.”

“Gotcha,” he replied. He tried to change the subject, “So...have you gotten someone else to be on your STEM team for the competition?”

I shook my head, “No.”

“Can I be on it?”

All of us stopped walking.

We turned and looked at Gavin.

"But I thought you hate math?" I said. "You didn't do well on the last test on simple machines, if I remember correctly."

"Yeah," Gavin paused.

"And you've always teased us for being good at math," I continued.

"I know, but I haven't done that in a while," Gavin raised his voice.

Marcus put his hand up at me as I almost jumped on Gavin, he turned to him, "Why is it you want to join us in the STEM competition? Sally's right. You complain about science and math all the time."

"Maybe in school. But you know I build things at my house. You've seen me work on my bike and my go-cart. I can be he lpful."

We looked at each other. Charlotte raised her eyebrows, "But Gavin it would mean being at school on a Saturday."

"I know it means I would be at school on Saturday. Maybe it would be fun to be in a competition."

I didn't know what to say. Never in a million-billion years thought I would be saying these words,

"Okay, Gavin, you can be on our STEM team."

Chapter 10 Turkey Sandwiches

Mom made turkey sandwiches for dinner. The sandwiches were easier for Jackson to pick up without making a mess. Jackson was able to pick up the sandwiches with one hand and stuff them in his mouth.

"There is nothing wrong with your jaw, Jackson. You can chew your food," Mom instructed.

Jackson put down the sandwich, and then he shot his left hand into the air, "I am ambidextrous!"

"No, you're not. You just ate a sandwich with your left hand, you're not ambidextrous," Michael rolled his eyes and took a bite of his sandwich.

"Am too!" Jackson replied

"Okay. Fine. You're ambidextrous," Michael replied.

"Stop arguing you two," said Dad.

"Sally, anymore news about the STEM competition?" Mom asked as she fed Austin in his chair.

I put my sandwich down, "Yes, actually. Gavin Eggleston wants to be on our team."

"Gavin Eggleston? You mean the boy that teases you and Charlotte about the Number Investigators?"

"The very one."

Mom furrowed her brow, "Why?"

I put my sandwich down, "He's been nicer to us since the math bee. And with his help with Charlotte's lemonade stand, he's been nicer. He doesn't get good school grades, but he did point out that he has worked on his bike and go-cart. Which I did know. So, we need a fourth person, and so I guess it will be Gavin."

"Well, just make sure he doesn't tease you or cause you any problems. Just let us know if he does," said Dad.

"I am sure he will be fine. Charlotte seems to be able to handle him when needed. He was scared of her today at school. Charlotte can handle him."

"Okay, then," Mom said.

"Are you guys going to get together and practice for the STEM competition?" Mom asked. I was confused, and it showed on my face. "Y'all aren't going to get together and build things?"

"But...you said I couldn't go over to my friends' houses, and they couldn't come over here for a week."

Mom looked at Dad, and they both looked at me.

"Well, I've been thinking about it. Maybe I, we, were a bit too hard on you about Jackson's arm. Broken arms happen. I was upset with the two of you running in the house. And to be honest, I am proud of the fact that you want to do this STEM competition. So, if you want to go over to Charlotte's to do a Number Investigators meeting, then that would be fine with us."

I squealed. This was not news I was expecting.

And it made my night.

Chapter 11 There's Been a Change

"I can come over this evening!" I shouted to Charlotte as we got on the bus that morning.

"That's a change. What happened?" she asked as we sat down.

"My parents said I could come over if we were working on things for the STEM competition."

"Okay, then, cool."

Later at recess, of all people, Gavin came running to me and Charlotte as we did our opening lap. "Are we going to get together and practice for the STEM competition?"

Charlotte and I looked at each other and furrowed our brows. I turned and spoke to Gavin,"Ummm... yeah...we are going to meet this afternoon at Charlotte's if you want to come. I wasn't expecting you to ask that."

"Well, if I am going to be a part of the team. I should be there to practice right?"

"Yes. I guess you should," replied Charlotte.

Marcus and Aaron came running to us. They were finishing their lap. They ran at full speed trying to beat each other.

"I win!" shouted Aaron. As they both passed us. They turned around and walked back to us. Both of them panting.

"What's going on?" Marcus asked, still breathing heavy.

"My parents changed their mind. I can come over to the tree house again," I informed him.

"That's a change," said Aaron.

"Mom felt bad. She wanted me to be able to get together and practice for the competition."

"That's awesome," said Marcus.

"Yeah, so we're going to meet this evening at Charlotte's to practice for the competition," Gavin piped up.

Marcus and Aaron went silent.

Marcus spoke first, "So...you're coming to Charlotte's to practice for the competition?"

"It was actually his idea," Charlotte replied, she smiled a little bit. I think she was a little proud at how Gavin had come around.

"Okay then!" Marcus smiled.

"So, if we do meet after school instead of our normal stuff, we need to bring things to build and make stuff with. Things that we could see in the competition," I said.

"Things like what?" Gavin asked over my shoulder.

"Oh...things...like tooth picks, marshmallows, pencils, empty cereal boxes, aluminum foil, things like that," I told him.

"Gotcha!"

"I think we can handle that," said Marcus. "Let's go, Aaron! I'll beat you to the monkey bars!" And off they ran.

We spent the rest of recess out chatting and climbing on the monkey bars.

Chapter 12 The First Practice

"Here ye! Here Ye! This Number Investigators meeting is now called to order," Charlotte pounded the floor of the treehouse with her gavel.

Marcus leaned over and took the gavel out of her hand, "Okay, seriously enough with the gavel. You're going to make a hole in the floor. And you're making my ears hurt."

Charlotte looked at her empty hand and shook her head at Marcus, "It's fun to use the gavel!"

"Apparently it is," he replied.

"Has anyone seen Gavin?" Charlotte asked.

"Nope," Marcus shook his head.

"I didn't," said Charlotte.

Aaron just shrugged his shoulders.

"I'm not expecting him to come," Marcus replied.

"It was his idea to come tonight," said Charlotte. "But he's not here, and we need to get started. Okay, my mom gave me some toothpicks and aluminum foil for us to use."

"I brought some tape. I know we'll need that," said Aaron holding up a roll of masking tape and roll of clear Scotch Tape.

"I brought tooth picks, marshmallows, and gum," I said showing my items.

"Gum?" Marcus asked.

"Yes, of course I brought gum. We can chew it and use it to make a sticky adhesive."

"Like glue or tape?" asked Aaron.

"Yes."

"Ewww!" the other three shouted.

"I'm not using someone else's chewed up gum for something sticky!" complained Aaron.

"I'm not saying use someone else's silly! And hey it works, don't knock it 'til you tried it! Of course, we can also just chew them if we want," I said.

"What are you all arguing about?" We heard someone climbing up the ladder.

I scooted over to the opening of the treehouse and looked down and saw Gavin climbing up the ladder with a brown grocery bag. He reached the top of the ladder and put the grocery bag into the treehouse. He pulled himself up, and he sat down in between me and Marcus.

"I brought some stuff for us to practice with!" Gavin moved the bag into the middle of the circle.

"What did you bring?" Charlotte asked.

"Here are a couple of shoe boxes, a packet of straws, some duct tape, pencils, and a few empty cereal boxes. Oh, and some Playdoh." He laid out his haul. The treehouse went quiet for a moment.

Marcus broke the silence. "Nice job, Gavin! Welcome!" He grinned and nodded his head as he inspected the items.

"What exactly are we going to build?" Gavin asked.

Charlotte looked at me, "Well, Sally, this is your project. What is it we are going to build?"

I raised a couple of sheets of paper with STEM projects that I found on the Internet. "Here are some ideas I found. These were projects other students made at other competitions. I thought maybe this is a good place to begin."

"What did you find? Is there one you are really interested in making?" Marcus asked without looking up from the treasures in front of him.

I flipped through the papers and found the one with the boat. I held it high in the air. "This one is about making a boat. It has to be able to float, travel across a container of water, and be able to hold a certain number of items, apparently some action figures."

"I like that idea! I'm going to run into the kitchen

and get a container of water." Charlotte got up and climbed down the ladder and went to her house

"It says it has to have action figures?" Marcus looked at the paper.

"It's says it has to carry four action figures. It looks like they would have been given that at the competition. I think that is how the competition at school is going to work. We will be given a challenge, and they will give us the items that go with the challenge. They should also get a planning sheet. Before we begin using the stuff they give us, we have to plan out our challenge. I don't know if that is how it is going to be at our school's competition, but that's seems to have happened at other school competitions."

"So, we would need to write down or plan what we are going to do?" Gavin asked.

"Yeah. At one school competition part of the group's score was their planning sheet," I said.

Gavin took a deep breath, "I don't always plan how to fix my bike or to work on my go-cart. When something needs to be fixed, I just tinker with it until it is fixed."

"I agree with you. I am just saying about what I what read about in a competition in Jefferson County," I motioned in the direction of Jefferson County.

The ladder rattled. Charlotte was climbing up the

ladder.

"How is she carrying a pan of water up the ladder?" Aaron asked.

Before I could look over the edge of the opening the treehouse, Charlotte's head popped up. She placed an empty plastic tub onto the floor. Then with the other hand, and some effort, she put a plastic jar of water on the floor. She pulled herself up the ladder.

"There's water in the lemonade pitcher, made it easier to carry it that way," she said. She moved the plastic tub into the middle of the treehouse. She poured the water from the pitcher into tub. The water hit the middle of the tube she stopped and put the jar down. "I guess that's about a half a gallon."

"Or two quarts," replied Aaron.

"Or eight cups," Marcus continued.

"Okay, you two you can stop that now," said Gavin.

"Don't you know how many quarts or cups are in a gallon?" asked Marcus.

"No," Gavin shot back.

"Marcus enough," I said, stopping the argument. I didn't have time for a fight between Gavin and the other boys. "This says to build a boat with a square foot of aluminum foil, a pencil, a piece of cloth, and a straw. And then place four action figures inside it."

"We don't have cloth or action figures," said Charlotte. "Do I need to go inside and get some of those things?"

"We can use the Play-doh for the action figures," said Gavin holding a container of green Play-doh.

"And we can use a piece of paper for the cloth. I am assuming the cloth would be used for something like the ship's sails," said Aaron. "We can be creative with the items we have. We don't always have to follow the instructions step by step."

"I agree," I replied. "And this is what it says 'You have to get your four action figures from one side of the ocean to other without the boat sinking, or tilting over, or losing any of the action figures. You can only use wind power."

"Wind power?" Gavin made a face.

"Meaning we have to blow on it to make it move." I said. I went back to explaining the expectations, "'You can use the materials in your packet. Aluminum foil, pencil, straw, cloth, string and tape. Good luck!' that's what the instructions that were given to a STEM competition said. I say we try and do that. Make a boat that doesn't sink and is able to carry the action figures we make across the tub of water."

"Sounds like plan to me," said Gavin.

We folded aluminum foil into an oblong bowl. We

used the pencils and attached them to the middle of the boat, making it stand up straight. Next, we took the straw and taped it across the pencil making a cross. We then attached the paper with tape to the pencil and straw cross, completing the sails for the boat.

"Cool," said Marcus.

I placed the boat in the water and then blew on at the paper. The boat actually moved.

"Well, that's cool," Gavin said, scooting closer to the tub.

"But we need to make the action figures and put them in the boat. That's where it gets more difficult. Put something in the boat to make sure it doesn't sink," I explained.

"One thing to remember, we don't have the original action figures that this contest used. There is no way for us to know how the figures we make would be compared to the action figures used in this example," said Aaron molding Play-Doh in his hands.

"Well of course, we wouldn't know. But I think the idea is to make a boat and for that boat to hold something as it goes across the water," replied Marcus as he also was molding Play-doh in his hands also making an action figure.

"Here toss me some," exclaimed Gavin. Aaron tossed him some Play-doh. And Charlotte finished off the Play-doh making the fourth action figure.

Marcus and Aaron made some fighting and explosion noises as they placed their hand made action figures into the boat. Charlotte and Gavin put their figures into the boat as well.

With all four figures in the boat, I blew at the paper sail. The boat moved, it tilted at first, but it made it across the tub.

"Look it sinks a little deeper into the water," Gavin pointed to side of the boat, noting that the boat was lower in the water.

"There's more weight in it with the figures," said Marcus.

"Obviously," replied Gavin with a hint of annoyance in his voice.

"Okay you two, don't fight," said Charlotte.

Gavin glared at Marcus and after a moment went back to playing with the Play-doh.

"Is there anything else we can build?" Aaron asked. "That assignment seemed pretty easy."

I looked at the other sheets.

"Why don't we just build with the stuff we have now. Do we need to follow an assignment Sally?" Charlotte asked.

Marcus joined in, "Yeah, let's look at what we have and get creative with that." He looked at the items in the middle of the treehouse.

I admit that sounded more fun, I realized that the other assignments I had printed off we didn't have all the correct items. Might as well just work on something we like. "Sure, that sounds fun," I replied.

We dug through the items we had.

"I'm going to make a suitcase," said Marcus.

"What do you mean?" replied Aaron who continued to handle Play-Doh.

Marcus took a shoebox, some Play-Doh, and tape. He formed a handle with the Play-Doh and taped it to the shoe box top. Next, he taped one side of the top to the box. He placed the box in front of him, and he opened the box. The taped side functioned like a hinge. "See!" Marcus said with pride.

"Gotcha!" replied Aaron.

We spent the next hour making different things with the random items we had brought. I worried that maybe we weren't practicing enough, but I didn't want to stop the fun.

Chapter 13 Who is Your Fourth Person?

"Get out your science journals," said Mrs. King. "And as you are getting those out, let me ask, how are the groups for the STEM competition? Is there anyone still missing someone for their group? The groups should be four people. Juan, Kadan do you have your four?"

"Yes, Kevin and Michael from Mrs. Smith's class are joining us to make our four," said Juan.

"That's good Juan. Sally, do you have your four?"

"Yes," I replied.

"Oh, who is your fourth person?" she raised her eyebrows.

"I am," Gavin raised his hand.

Mrs. King looked stunned, then composed herself. "Well, good for you Gavin. I am glad to see you giving this a try."

A few chuckles went up around the room, but Mrs. King gave them "The Look" and they shut right up. She turned and looked at me, "Good Sally, I am glad to see you have a group. I look forward to seeing what you come up with."

During recess, I was finishing my lap around the track, Mrs. King called me, "Sally, come here for a moment."

I looked at Charlotte, "Uh-oh, I wonder what this is about!"

"Good luck!" Charlotte yelled at me as I ran toward Mrs. King.

"Yes, Mrs. King?"

"So, tell me about Gavin. I wouldn't have ever expected him to be your fourth person," Mrs. King seemed genuinely impressed. "How is he doing? Is he doing okay? Is he bothering you all?"

"He wasn't what I was expecting either. But he overheard us saying we needed a fourth person, and he wanted to do it. He works a lot on his bike, so he could be useful when it comes to building things." I was nervous, I kept standing up on my tip-toes and then coming back down again.

"Okay, well, that's good. As long as he is behaving himself, then by all means go for it. Now go play." And with that, she sent me away to play.

Chapter 14 Practice at School

The class sat in a circle around the blue rug, and Mrs. King sat underneath the Smartboard and began the meeting.

"Okay, for those in the STEM competition, today during science you will be in the cafe with Mrs. Russell. She will discuss the competition and she will give you a practice problem to work on," said Mrs. King.

"I didn't know we would be working on STEM stuff today," I spoke without raising my hand.

Mrs. King did not like me talking out of turn. I could tell by the look on her face. "Mrs. Russell came to me this morning to ask to see the STEM competitors. So, I didn't know about it until this morning, sometimes we teachers come up with an idea that we have to do, and we think of it on the way to school. I think Mrs. Russell had an idea that she just had to do with the group."

"Gotcha," I replied.

"How long are we going to be out of class?" Gavin asked.

Mrs. King paused and stared at Gavin for a moment before she could speak, "I know you're excited about getting out of class Gavin, but it will only be for about forty minutes. Mrs. Russell's class will be in art during that time, but you will meet her in the cafe. I think she has it planned. You all will work on some projects there."

"So, it will be like we get two resources today," Gavin pumped his fist.

Mrs. King paused again before replying to Gavin, "Yes. I guess those of you who are on the STEM team do get two resources today."

A grin broke across my face. Gavin looked at me and raised both his fist in the air, "Yes!" he exclaimed.

"Calm down, Gavin," Mrs. King told him. "Now, let's begin our Morning Meeting."

We did our Morning Meeting talking about sitting with different people at lunch, especially those that don't seem to have friends. But I like my friends, and they're not any new people in our class, so I don't understand why we talk about things we don't need to deal with. But I guess, if someone new were to come into the class Charlotte and I would talk with them to see if they were nice.

Later, that morning Mrs. King sent me, Charlotte, Marcus, Gavin, Juan and Kadan to the cafeteria. Gavin and Marcus grinned the whole walk down the hallway, they were just so excited to get out of science. I had never seen the two of them smile in each other's presence before. Getting out of class gave them something to bond over, I guess.

Michael and Kevin in Juan's group were already there.

We walked into the cafeteria. Mrs. Russell had several blue bins filled with different things spread out on different tables.

"Come on in," Mrs. Russell waved to us.

The other grades were already there. The fourth and fifth grade team were already sitting. "Sally, Charlotte, Gavin, and Marcus go and sit at the purple table." She pointed to a sign written in purple. "Juan, your group will sit over at the green table."

Mrs. Russell waited for us to sit before she continued, "Thank you guys and gals for coming to see me."

"We got out of science!" said Gavin.

Mrs. Russell smiled at him, "Yes, Gavin we know." She turned back to the rest of the group. "Now, on the tables in front of you are your buckets. In your buckets you will find the instructions for the project." She raised a sheet of paper like the one we had in our bucket. "You will also find the items listed in the assignment. Today you will find Legos, small pieces of cardboard, and some string."

"Legos!" shouted several people, and few people clapped.

"Yes, Legos, keep your focus on me. They may give you Legos at the competition, you need to not freak out and get all excited about the Legos and forget to do what the problem is instructing you to solve. So, let's go ahead and read our problem. This is how the competition will go. I will read the problem out loud, follow along." Mrs. Russell looked at the paper and started to read, "Okay architects, the town of Sweetville needs a library that is two stories tall and can allow people in wheelchairs to get to the second floor. Using the Legos, the Lego figure, cardboard, and string, build a building that allows the figure in the wheelchair access to all the floors, and the ability to get around to the bookshelves. Use the paper and pencils provided to plan out your building."

Mrs. Russell looked up from the paper, "So, on the day of the competition you get points based on how well you plan and work together, not just if you finish the project correctly. You will earn points for planning, working together, and completing the project correctly."

"Who is going to be grading us?" Sanjey asked.

"Good question. There will be teachers and volunteers from all three schools. The competition will be in the gym, because it has more room. Tables will be spread out, but they will be roped off. Parents can see you and walk around, but they can't get really close."

"Or they'll give us help," shouted Gavin.

"Yes, Gavin that is the point. We don't want the people watching to be giving help. But we also need the room for the teachers to come by and see your work. It would be very hard to do that if they were being blocked by all the parents watching."

"How many points can we earn?" asked Marcus.

"Good question Marcus. Sixty. You get twenty points for each section as I mentioned before--Planning Together, Working Together, and Successful Completion of the Project. So, I want you to understand there is more than just getting the project correct. It is about working together as a team." She looked around the room, I think she was making sure we understood. "Are there any more questions? Because if there are no more questions, we can begin our practice project here." She looked around the room one last time. "Okay, you have twenty minutes, and go!"

I grabbed the instructions and looked them over one more time. Gavin began to take out all the Legos.

"Let's sort them by size," said Marcus.

"Yeah, that way we can see how many pieces we have," replied Charlotte. "And here is the cardboard and string." She put five small pieces of cardboard and the string in a pile to the side.

"What's the string for?" asked Gavin.

"Not sure yet," I said.

I put down the instructions and pulled out the planning paper and grabbed a pencil. "Okay, we know we have to have two floors. The guy in the wheelchair," I held up the figure, "has to be able to get into the building and has to be able to get to the second floor of the library and back down to the first floor of the library."

Marcus stacked several Legos together. It looked like he was building a wall.

Charlotte stopped him, "Marcus! I know you want to build with the Legos, but we don't have the time to build and figure it out as we go. We need to discuss the plan first."

Marcus made a face, "You're right," and he put the wall of Legos to the side.

Charlotte picked one of the cardboard pieces, "Obviously, I think these are for ramps. Since I don't see any pieces of ramps in the Lego section."

"They make ramps in Legos, why didn't they give us one?" Gavin wondered.

Everyone rummaged through the Legos.

"Well, there don't seem to be any ramps, here," said Charlotte.

"I don't know why they wouldn't give us ramps. But this is what we have to work with," I replied.

"Do we have to use the string?" Marcus asked.

I looked at the instructions again, "No, I don't see any rule that says we have use the string."

"Yeah, I'm not sure what we would use the string for," Marcus said.

"The string could be used as part of an elevator!" shouted Gavin. He grabbed a couple of bricks quickly put together a square and wrapped the string around the top of square. "We put the figure in the elevator and then we can pull up the elevator and the figure." Gavin demonstrated by lifting the square with the figure in the wheelchair up.

We all looked at Gavin, and then we looked at each other. "Gavin, that's actually a really good idea with the string. Let's hold onto that, if we need it. Good job. But we still need to plan out the building," said Marcus, he patted Gavin on the back, and Gavin smiled. "But the main thing we need are ramps," Marcus grabbed a cardboard piece and laid it across a small Lego, he then rolled the figure up the cardboard. He released it and it rolled back down.

Gavin grabbed the other cardboard pieces and laid them out in front of him, "We need one for the front door. We need one to get from the first floor to the second floor. And we would need a couple for a fire escape."

"I would have never thought of the fire escape," I said.

"Does it say anything about making a fire escape?" Charlotte asked.

"No, but I think it's a pretty cool idea though," I replied.

I took the planning paper and drew out an idea for the first floor. "Here is the front door, and here is where we can put the ramp to go up to the second floor."

"Don't forget to put shelves for the books," Marcus said.

"Good point, I forgot that," I quickly drew a couple of rectangles representing shelves. Next, I sketched out my idea for the second floor, "And here is what we can do with the second floor, it matches where the first ramp comes up. And here is a door for the emergency exit. Any questions or other ideas? We're running out of time."

"I like this plan," Marcus smiled and began stacking Legos.

"Looks good to me," Gavin said.

"Let's get this done," Charlotte instructed.

We worked quickly. Gavin seemed to be in charge of placing the cardboard ramps. Which was fine by me. He was the one that sorted them and came up with the idea for the emergency exit. Marcus and I worked on the walls of the building, and Charlotte made the shelves for the imaginary books.

"You have five minutes," Mrs. Russell called out.

"Man, that was quick," I said.

We finished working on the emergency ramp. I then ran the figure up and down the ramps, making it sure it worked.

"Okay, time! Step away from your buildings," Mrs. Russell spoke in her loud voice. We stepped away from our table.

Mrs. Russell started with the groups that were farthest from us on the other side of the room. "I want everyone, to gather around each project so we can see it and discuss how each group worked on their project. So, come on over here by Kevin, Sam, Jake, and Karen's group." We gathered around the table. Kevin's group was fourth graders. Their building looked a little like ours, but they didn't have a fire escape. "So, Kevin, or whoever in this group that wants to show us how the figure can get into the building.

"See, he can fit here between the shelves and the wall," Kevin moved the figure around the bookshelf.

Charlotte, Marcus, and Gavin looked at me with worry in their eyes. "We didn't check that!" Charlotte whispered to me.

"We're we supposed to do that?" Marcus whispered in my ear.

"The figure in the wheelchair is supposed to be able to see the books on the bookshelf. She said it before during the instructions," Gavin whispered in my ear.

I didn't say anything. All I could think of was everyone looking at our building and seeing that our figure in the wheelchair can't get around the building to even see the all the bookshelves. We possibly built a library where he could get in and out of, not be able to see the books that were in the library.

"Okay, Kevin show us how the figure gets down to the first floor, since you started him on the second floor," instructed Mrs. Russell.

"By using this ramp," Kevin let the figure slid down a cardboard ramp. It was the same idea we used.

"Cool," replied Mrs. Russell. "Now how does he get out?"

"Like this," Kevin reached his finger through a hole in the wall, that looked to be a window. He pushed the figure out the door and it rolled out onto the table.

"Nicely done you all! Now does anyone have any questions?" asked Mrs. Russell.

Marcus raised his hand.

"Yes, Marcus?"

"Is the figure supposed to be able to make it around the shelf?"

Mrs. Russell made a face, and then fixed it, "Of course, Marcus, the person needs to be able to get into the library and see the books. That's the point of going to the library. Did your group forget that? It's in the instructions."

The rest of group looked at me. I felt sick to my stomach. "Y'all heard and had the instructions too! Why didn't you guys check?" I whispered back to them.

"Let's look at fifth grade next," said Mrs. Russell. She walked to their table and we all followed. "Sanjey, why don't you show us your library."

Sanjey was the winner of the Turing Math Bee, he beat out all of us Number Investigators. Charlotte won the whole third grade. It would be my bet he and his group could win the STEM competition as well, he is very good at this stuff.

"Well, our library has two stories," said Sanjey. Stories in this case means floors. "We have an entrance here in the front. Another entrance in the back, and then we have a fire escape coming from the top floor."

Charlotte elbowed me and whispered, "See we can think of things like Sanjey can."

"Or maybe he stole it from us," whispered Gavin with a smile on his face.

"Nicely done, Sanjey. Madison can you show us how the figure gets around?" asked Mrs. Russell.

Madison Berkley had blond curly hair and was very pretty. She was also very smart. She took the figure and put it on the first ramp, "He can roll into the library like this, and then he can see this first bookshelf." She moved around to the other of the building and reached in through a window, "And then he can come around to this side of the bookshelf." She pushed the figure around the bookshelf. "And then he can get up to the second floor with either the ramp or the elevator, which we can pull with the string."

Gavin grinned and elbowed me in the ribs, "I told you!" Gavin kept grinning and he nodded his head as he turned to look at Madison moving their figure around.

"That's excellent with the elevator," exclaimed Mrs. Russell.

Madison moved their elevator and pushed the figure out onto the second floor. She maneuvered it around the bookshelves. "Nicely done fifth grade!" said Mrs. Russell. "Okay, third grade you're up. Show us what you have, let's start with Juan's group."

We stood over Juan's Lego building. Juan pushed

the figure through the front opening of their library, and he pushed it around. The figure made it easily around the floor and bookshelves. I was jealous and nervous all at the same time. Their library worked.

"Good you guys. Okay, Sally, show us your library," Mrs. Russell smiled and waved us on to our table.

I picked up the figure and placed him next to the front door. "He can get into the library this way, by using the ramp." I pushed him into the front door. I could feel everyone looking at me as the figure went into the first floor.

"Wonderful, now can he get around to the bookshelves? It looks a little tight in there," Mrs. Russell squatted down next to our library and looked through the front door.

I stuck my finger into the window and pushed the figure. He wouldn't move. He wouldn't fit between the shelf Charlotte had made and the wall. We only left one Lego bump space.

Mrs. Russell stood up, "Okay everyone, what can third grade do differently? What can we learn from this?"

Sanjey raised his hand, "They only gave one space between the wall and the bookshelf. They should use at least three."

I felt my face turn red.

"Sally, do you all understand that?" asked Mrs. Russell.

The four of us nodded our heads. "Yes, ma'am," we replied.

Gavin shouted out, "But our figure can get to the second floor by using the ramp! Show them."

I pushed the figure away from the bookshelf and up the ramp.

"Nicely done you all," said Mrs. Russell.

"Is that a fire escape?" asked Sanjey pointing to the ramp.

"Yes, it is!" replied Marcus.

I pushed the figure out the side door and let it slide all the way down.

Sanjey nodded his head, "Very cool!"

"That is cool," said Madison.

"Nicely done third grade," said Mrs. Russell. "I like the addition of the fire escape as well. That's a nice touch." She clapped her hands, "Okay, nicely done everyone. Our quick time is up. I wanted to do quick run of an actual problem that had been used at another STEM competition. Please break apart your Lego creations and put them back in the tubs and put the string and cardboard back in as well. Then sit for a just a second."

We put away our stuff and sat as we were told.

"What did you all think of the problem today?" Mrs. Russell asked.

Sanjey raised his hand, "It took a while to figure out what to do with the string."

"True. I noticed that fifth grade was the only one to use it in their library. Which is fine. There was no instruction that said you had to use the string. They may do that. Put some material in there that isn't quite clear about how to use, to see what you come up with. Now if the instructions say you are required to use certain material, then use it. But remember the focus needs to be on solving the problem."

"Why didn't we get ramps? There are ramps in Lego sets," Marcus asked.

Mrs. Russell laughed, "That's only because the set I have didn't come with ramps." She continued to laugh, "But Marcus, in a way it was a good exercise because you just don't know what you will be given, and you will need to adapt. And work with your team when adapting, and then record it in your plans. But it seems no one here seemed to freak out about the fact there were no official Lego ramps in the bins. Am I correct?" she held up her hands as she looked around the room.

"We did a little," said Gavin.

"But you all clearly didn't let it stop you. In fact, you and Sanjey's group were the only ones that had a fire escape, not having official ramps didn't stop you. By the way, good job on that third grade. Well, I love spending time with you all, but I need to go get my class, and you all need to head on back to yours. I will talk with you all on Friday, so we can be ready for the competition this Saturday."

We stood up and headed back to class.

"Good job with the emergency exit, that was a great idea," said Juan as we walked down the hall.

"Thanks," I replied. "But you didn't make our mistake though."

"That's what that meeting was for, to make mistakes and learn from them. To practice a little. Don't sweat it," said Kadan.

"Well, that was fun. I want to continuing working with Legos as opposed to going to math now," said Gavin.

"I'm with you man," replied Marcus. "Is there a Number Investigators meeting tonight?"

"I guess if you want to have one," said Charlotte.

"Do you all want to have one?"

"I would like to have one," I said.

"Yeah, let's have one tonight!" replied Gavin.

"Cool," replied Marcus.

Charlotte and I looked at each other, Marcus and Gavin were becoming friends.

Chapter 15 Where is Gavin?

"Here ye! Here Ye! Let's begin this Number Investigators meeting," shouted Charlotte. She pounded her gavel; the treehouse made the noise louder.

Marcus reached out and grabbed it, "Okay, okay, again with the gavel." And he placed it to the side, with a very large eye roll.

It was me, Charlotte, Marcus, and Aaron at the meeting. We had brought a lot of things for us to practice making for the STEM competition. It all sat in the middle of us – plastic tubs filled with Legos, Magnix, string, tape, paper, some paper towel rolls, action figures, aluminum foil, and other random things our parents let us take out of houses.

"Where's Gavin?" Marcus asked.

"I don't know," Charlotte replied. "Did you remind him to come?"

"Well, aren't we going to practice for the STEM competition?" Marcus said. "I mean I told him to be here."

"Wait! Gavin is supposed to be coming," asked Aaron.

"Yeah, after STEM practice today he said he was coming," I said.

"Well, I don't think we're working on any math homework tonight, are we?" asked Charlotte.

Marcus held up a box of Legos, "You would rather work on math homework over building with Legos?"

"I wanted to practice for the STEM competition tonight," I said. "It is this weekend after all."

"Well, what do you want to make?" Charlotte asked.

I pulled out a STEM problem I printed off the internet. I waved it in the air, "This one is about making soda straw rockets."

"You have my attention," said Marcus, as he scooted to face me.

I showed the plans, "The idea is we design a rocket with paper that can be launched from blowing through a straw. The winner is the one who can get their rocket to go the farthest."

"Did you bring straws?" asked Charlotte.

I reached into the tub in front of me, grabbed the box of straws and held them up, "Yup."

"I like this project," said Aaron. "Can I help, even though I won't be there Saturday?"

"Of course you can," I replied. "Everyone take a straw." I held out the box. "This is an individual project. We each build our own rocket, and then we can discuss how they work."

Suddenly, the treehouse began to shake. The ladder moved. "I'm coming up, I'm here," shouted Gavin as he made the climb up the tree.

We stared at the door to the treehouse as we waited for him to come in the door. He flung a backpack into the treehouse. It made a noise that made it sound like there were a ton of things in it. He climbed in.

I moved the backpack away from the front door, it was very heavy. "What's in here," I asked.

"Let me show you," he took the bag and unzipped it. "I brought some rolls of duct tape, a hammer, nails, and some pieces of wood."

"Why?" I asked.

"To make things," Gavin replied. "Aren't we here to make things? It looks like you don't want me to bring this?"

I shook my head. "Yes, you can bring it. But I don't think they're going to give us stuff like this...."

"Stuff for a wood shop class," Aaron replied.

"Well, we'll put stuff together with the things you brought later. We were just about to make some straw rockets," Marcus explained.

Gavin looked disappointed. I tried to make him feel better, "Gavin, it's cool that you brought all of this stuff. But this straw rocket is an example from another STEM competition. It's things like this that more than likely we will be making."

"Okay, let's make a straw rocket," Gavin said, he seemed to deflate like a balloon.

"Take a straw," he took one out of my hand. "The idea is using regular copy paper and tape, we make a rocket. We blow through the straw and that launches the rocket. The person whose rocket goes furthest will win. There are some basic instructions here. We need to cut each paper so that it will wrap around the straw, but not be so tight that it won't fly off the straw when we blow. We also need to add fins to make sure the rocket flies straight. It also shows that we need to make a cone or a tip on the rocket, or it will catch some air as it flies."

"Okay, this would be cool to do in class, especially when class gets boring," said Gavin. He took a piece of paper and started to cut the paper. I finished passing out paper to the rest of the club. I put the instructions in the middle of the treehouse. For the next few minutes we spent time cutting, wrapping, and taping pieces of paper around the straws.

Marcus finished first. "I'm ready, let's do this." He held his straw with the rocket straight up. One by one, the rest of us finished.

"I guess we need to line up together and that way we can tell who's rocket goes the furthest," I said. We all scooted to one side of the treehouse. I looked at the rest of the club, "Okay ready? On three. One, two, three..." and we puffed on our straws and our paper rockets shot off.

Mine went straight. Marcus's went straight down and crashed. Charlotte's went straight, but spiraled as it flew. Aaron's did well, it flew straight and smooth, and hit the far wall of the treehouse. Gavin's did a loop de loop and landed four feet in front of him.

"I won!" shouted Aaron. Of course he won, the one person in our group that isn't going to be with us in the competition.

"It's a shame you won't be with us on Saturday," said Charlotte.

"Sally's did well, and so did yours," Aaron replied.

"Why did mine crash?" asked Marcus as he picked his rocket up. He held it up and examined it.

Charlotte looked over his shoulder, "It looks like your fins are all different sizes. Maybe that had something to do with it. They should all be the same size. Look at the plans." She picked up the instructions and showed them to Marcus.

"Also, maybe the tape got stuck on the straw," said Gavin.

"You do have a lot of tape on your rocket. He may be right," explained Aaron as he examined the rocket.

Marcus looked at Gavin, "Maybe a better question is how did yours do a loop de loop?"

Gavin laughed, he picked up his rocket and looked at it. "Maybe it was the front here. I didn't close it well. It could have caught some air and held the front end up." He tilted the front of his rocket back and showed it flipping backwards. "I think the front of mine just needed to be closed better than it was."

"I want to try again," said Marcus as balled up his rocket and grabbed another piece of paper. He got to work.

"So, do I. I want to beat you guys," said Gavin.

So, we all tried again. Marcus was more careful with his rocket, and Gavin seemed to triple check the cone of his rocket this time. We all took longer making our rockets this time, double checking fins, tape, and the cones at the front of the rockets.

We lined up once more and puffed on our straws. None of the rockets crashed or did a loop de loop this time. They all flew straight and smooth.

And mine hit the far wall of the treehouse. It was the only one. So, I won.

"Oh! Come on!" shouted Gavin. He threw his

hands into the air.

"Go Sally! Go Sally!" danced Charlotte.

"Why thank you!" and I took a deep bow.

"Okay, try again," said Marcus.

We did several more rounds of launching rockets. Each time trying harder to make sure the rockets were perfect.

After three more rocket launches, where Charlotte won twice, and Aaron won once more, Gavin barked his frustration, "I am never going to win this! If this is the type of thing we're going to do in the competition, we are going to lose!"

"Dude! Chill!" shouted Marcus. "Not that big a deal. Okay, let's do something else."

"I want to hammer something," seethed Gavin.

"Okay, let's get out the wood and nails you brought and hammer the nails into that," I said.

"Good idea," agreed Charlotte.

We spent the rest of the evening pounding nails into wood.

I hoped Gavin wasn't going to throw a fit at the competition.

Chapter 16 Are We Having Another Meeting?

It was Friday the 23rd, one day before the competition. Charlotte and I were outside walking a lap around the track to start recess.

"How do you think we're going to do tomorrow?" Charlotte asked.

"I have no idea to be honest. We've never done this before," I replied. "Gavin can do well, but it will depend on his mood. Will he get upset and get frustrated? And then completely and totally embarrass us? I don't know."

"Well, it's supposed to be for fun," Charlotte replied.

"But it is a competition! And how would you feel if someone told you that the math bee is supposed to be just for fun?" I said. I was a little mean.

Charlotte took a deep breath, "You're right. You're right. I would be mad if someone told me that. But really, the only thing we can do is to go into the competition and just do our best. We've practiced a lot, and we know the steps of STEM. That's why I said, just have some fun with it. There is nothing more you can do to prepare for it. So, just have fun now."

I heard Marcus and Aaron running behind us.

They raced each other around the track. Aaron zoomed past us and threw his hands into the air, "Whoo- hoo! I win."

Marcus came running up two seconds later, "Dang it!" he shouted as he ran passed us.

"You're getting slow," said Aaron as he turned around. He was breathing heavy.

"You getting excited about tomorrow?" Marcus asked as he slowed his breathing.

"I'm getting nervous," I replied.

"Why? We'll be fine," Marcus waved me off. I rolled my eyes.

Gavin came up behind us, "Are we meeting to-night?" he asked.

"I don't know," I said. "Do you want to?"

"Are you bringing a nail gun if we do?" Aaron asked.

"Very funny," Gavin shot back.

"Because that would be awesome if you did bring a nail gun," said Marcus. "Bang! Bang!" Marcus pre-tended to be shooting a gun.

"Nail guns aren't actual guns. You know that, right?" Gavin said glaring at Marcus.

"They shoot nails, don't they?" replied Marcus.

Gavin shook his head, turned his back to Marcus, and walked away down to the playground. He turned back and shouted, "So are we having a meeting then tonight at Charlotte's? At the treehouse?"

Charlotte looked at me, "It's fine by me."

"I guess so then," I replied to Gavin. And he turned around and ran towards the playground.

"I hope he does well tomorrow, and doesn't kill anybody," said Marcus.

"So do I," I replied.

Chapter 17 The STEM T-shirt

"Come on in Sally's group," Mrs. Russell waved at us. All the other teams were already there, including Juan's. We seem to have a habit of being last to these meetings. "Pick a table to sit at." The four of us sat down at a table close to the window, the chairs were really close to ground. I couldn't believe I was this short in Kindergarten.

Mrs. Russell held up a white t-shirt with the words Turing Elementary STEM Competition written across the front in big blue and red lettering. "I have your t-shirts for tomorrow. You will need to wear these when you come to school tomorrow. It will let the volunteers know to let you come back here to my room, which is where we will meet. Remember to be here at 9 a.m. tomorrow, the competition will begin at 9:30, so we will need you to be here then to so we can get ready."

"How are you getting here?" I whispered to Gavin.

His faced turned red, and I felt embarrassed, "Marcus's family is going to take me. So, don't worry about me."

"Don't worry Sally. We got him," whispered Marcus.

"Okay everyone, we don't have a lot of time. Just a few reminders, there will be two other schools here.

So, there will be students and teachers here that you don't know. Also, the gym will be set-up with tables. Parents will be able to walk around, but they won't be able to stand next your table because your tables will be roped off."

Chapter 18 Last Treehouse Meeting

"Here ye! Here ye! This meeting of the Number Investigators is called to order," Charlotte pounded her gavel.

Marcus covered his ears, but this time didn't take the gavel.

We sat in the middle of Charlotte's treehouse, the sun came in through the openings giving us light. I like the spring with the longer sunlight in the evenings. Aaron came as well, and he was still dressed in his baseball uniform, dirt spread over his knees. Even Gavin was there on time. We had left the stuff in the middle of the treehouse from our meeting last night, including Gavin's backpack with the nails, wood, and hammer.

"I suggest we take a vote on what we want to work on this evening," said Marcus looking at me.

I was hurt at the suggestion.

"Why? What if Sally wants to work on something specific? This STEM competition is kinda her thing. She wanted to lead this," Charlotte told him.

I was afraid Charlotte was going to going kill him, so I swallowed my pride and asked, "Is there something you want to work on Marcus?"

Marcus shrugged his shoulders, "I want to build something with the wood pieces Gavin has. And actually build something, not just bang nails into the blocks." He picked up the piece of wood that we practiced on last night. The nails made it look like a porcupine.

"Well, let's see what I have in here," Gavin picked up his bag, and took out the remaining pieces of wood. He counted as he pulled them out of the bag. "One, two, three..." and he placed them in the middle of us. He kept going, "eight, nine, and ten. I brought ten pieces. I agree, I think we can make something of this."

The pieces were all different lengths and sizes. Marcus reached in, picked up two of the longest pieces and held them straight up and down. "We could build a field goal." He made the sounds of a football being kicked into the air and then the crowd cheering.

"That wouldn't be tall enough," said Aaron.

"And I have no interest in making a field goal," I replied. I put air quotes around the words field goal.

"I agree with her," said Charlotte.

Gavin raised his hand, "What about a box to hold our stuff in. We could keep the math stuff here in the treehouse if we built a box. I'll show you. Here, Marcus, give me those pieces."

"We're really not going to do the field goal idea?"

Marcus looked disappointed.

"No," Gavin replied. "Now give me the pieces, please."

Marcus frowned and handed the pieces to Gavin. Gavin laid the pieces down on the floor, in order of height, "We take these two pieces. They will be the long sides of the box, and then we take these pieces, lay them down flat and they become the bottom of the box. These other pieces we use to build up the side." He did his best to hold the pieces in place.

"That piece is a little long, see it stick out past the other pieces," Aaron pointed to the piece.

Gavin's face lit up, "I can solve that! I'll run home and get my saw."

"You have an electric saw?" Aaron asked.

Gavin rolled his eyes, "I'm not bringing my electric saw! This can be done with just a regular hand saw. You all start putting together the pieces together. I'll be right back."

And Gavin bolted out the treehouse and down the ladder. The treehouse shook as he bounced down the ladder.

Aaron looked at Gavin, "Was it me? Or did he imply that he has an actual electric saw?"

"He did," Marcus nodded his head, impressed.

I actually liked this idea of the box. It wasn't what I thought we were going to do. "Let's put together the bottom part of the box first," I said. I gently put the other pieces to the side, but kept them in order. "We should put these two pieces together, and then we can put the other pieces up as the sides."

"Good idea," replied Aaron.

Marcus grabbed two nails and the hammer. I held one block on the floor and Aaron held the other one next it. Marcus hammered the two nails into the pieces at an angle. He held them up, they seemed to be a little loose, but they held.

The ladder began to shake as we heard Gavin headed back into the treehouse.

"He must have sprinted with that saw in his hand," said Aaron.

"I'm glad the police didn't see him flying down the street with a saw in his hand," laughed Marcus.

"I just hope he doesn't fall as he comes up the ladder and seriously hurt himself with it," said Charlotte.

Gavin climbed into the treehouse, and he put the saw into the middle of the room. It clanged as it hit the floor.

"You ran with that?" Marcus pointed at the saw.

Gavin looked at the saw, and then at Marcus, "Yeah?"

Marcus closed his eyes and shook his head, "Okay."

Gavin shrugged him off, "I also brought some wood glue." He pulled the tan colored bottle out of his back pocket and held it up. "I see you already tried to nail the bottom parts of the box together." He pointed at the two pieces.

"Yeah, but it's a little loose," said Charlotte showing him the two pieces moving slightly even though there were two nails jammed into them.

"That's what's the wood glue is for," said Gavin. He took the pieces from Charlotte and opened the bottle and squirted a very thin strip of glue between the two blocks. He pushed together and held them firmly for a moment. "If these were bigger pieces, there's a vise that I would use to hold these together until the glue completely set. But this should work for our purposes." He pushed a little more and put the pieces down on the floor.

Gavin took over. He directed us building the box, telling us which piece should go where. He allowed us to take turns using the hammer or using the wood glue.

He took the longer piece that needed to have an inch or so cut off, the piece that Aaron noticed was longer than the others. He laid it across the side of the box where he wanted it to go. "Okay, we want to make sure we only cut once, so to make sure that happens we need to measure it twice."

"Which is what the phrase measure twice-cut once, refers too," said Charlotte.

"Yup," continued Gavin pointing at Charlotte. "We can measure it by laying the piece across the side where we want it to go. And then we can take a pencil to mark on the piece where we want to cut." He made a line with his pencil. "Then normally I would lay the board across two saw horses, but since we don't have room for them here, let's put the wood box on top of this box." He grabbed a plastic tub that held other pieces for STEM, and he put the wood box on top of it. "This gives me some room to cut." The board was now almost a foot off the floor. He put his left hand in the middle of the board and with his right hand he held the saw. He made sure the saw was in contact with the pencil line he drew. And then he cut. He held out his tongue as he cut. He made four quick cuts and the piece fell to the floor. He picked up the board, blew off the remaining saw dust and wiped it with his hand. He laid the piece back on top of the wood box, "See, now it matches."

"Now I want to cut things," Marcus said. He held up the piece Gavin had cut off.

Charlotte took the hammer and a nail, "Can I hammer it in?"

"Go ahead," Gavin got out of the way.

Charlotte made quick work of the nail, hitting it twice before the nail was completely in.

"Nicely done," said Aaron.

For the next few minutes, we took turns hammering in nails and using the wood glue to make sure the pieces stayed in place.

Gavin handed me the box. "Take a look. That's some pretty good woodwork there," he smiled. "It is definitely building something."

I nodded my head, "I agree." I held up the box. It was neat. The sides were smooth, and no pieces seemed to stick out. "We had to use some math, measuring to make sure it was put together correctly."

"And Gavin used some engineering to cut the board to see that it fit else," said Marcus.

"Well, that's definitely at least two of the STEM parts, so if we're asked tomorrow to build something, I know we can do it."

There was a loud crash. Magnix pieces were all over the floor. Aaron held up a couple of pieces, "We've made one thing, let's work on some others."

And we spent the next little while building with the Magnix set.

"It's 7:30, I need to head home," said Aaron.

"Me too," Gavin added.

I threw my hands up in the air like a traffic cop. "Wait! Before any goes remember that you have to where your STEM shirt."

"Mine's folded and sitting on top of my dresser," Charlotte said.

"I'll remember," replied Marcus.

"I got mine ready," said Gavin.

"And I'll make sure he has it," continued Marcus.

"What do you mean?" I asked.

"He's picking me up tomorrow and taking me there. My dad has to work," said Gavin.

"Oh, okay," I felt bad. It never occurred to me that Gavin may not have a way to get to school. So, it's even better now that Marcus and Gavin seem to be becoming friends.

Chapter 19 The STEM Competition

As we pulled into the parking lot of the school, I saw the huge sign announcing welcoming Holly Hills and Cedarwood Road Elementary schools to the STEM contest. The parking lot was halfway full. I got out of the car, and Charlotte pulled up next to us.

"Hey! We're here," she smiled as she got out of the back of her car wearing her STEM t-shirt.

"There are more people here than I was expecting," I said looking at the cars that were driving into the lot.

"It is three schools," Charlotte said matter-of-factly. "It will fine!" she patted me on the back. "Plus, it will be fun, don't forget that! This will be fun!"

"Yes! It will be a lot of fun having all those people staring back at you!" Michael snarked at me.

"Michael! Be nice to your sister!" said Dad.

"Yes, Michael, stop being mean to Sally!" ordered Jackson, his five-year-old voice was cute when he tried to be bossy.

"You tell 'em Jackson," Dad nodded his head.

When we got into the school, signs told people where to go – parents to the cafeteria, participants to

Mrs. Russell's room.

Charlotte and I headed towards Mrs. Russell's classroom.

"Hello girls!" Mrs. Russell smiled. She wore her STEM T-shirt, but hers had Coach written on the back. "The rest of your teammates aren't here yet, but I have a table labeled for you." She pointed to a table covered in ABCs. We sat in the short chairs.

The hallway grew noisy.

"The other schools are meeting in the rooms next us," Mrs. Russell said pointing to the hallway.

"Where are they, Marcus and Gavin?" I leaned over to Charlotte.

Marcus and Gavin bounded into the room.

"Whew!" I whispered to myself.

"Boys, glad to see you, go find your team," Mrs. Russell waved her hand in our direction.

"I bet you thought we weren't going to be here?" said Marcus as he sat down.

I shook my head, "No. I figured you would be here."

"Yeah, you didn't think I would be here. But I want to win," said Gavin.

Mrs. Russell clapped her hands twice, and we repeated the clap and got quiet. "Okay, thanks everyone for giving me your attention. When we get out there into the gym remember you will see a table with your team's name. So, go and gather there. Remember that I will make an announcement, then some teachers from the other schools will announce the project. Next some volunteers will come by and give you the stuff you need for the project. After the time is up, someone will announce the winners. Don't forget different people will be coming by and watching you, making notes of how you are working together as a team, as well as planning and executing the project. Remember, you don't just get points for finishing or completing the task. So, let's all line up and follow me. It's time for us to head to the gym."

Mrs. Russell led us down the hallway. Some of the hallway was roped off and the parents were behind the rope. Parents cheered their child as they walked past. I think I may have heard Michael scream my name. But I was too nervous to look for him. I wished I was able to chew bubble gum. It would have helped with my nerves. I noticed I was chewing my tongue instead as we reached the gym. I saw our table. It had all four of our names on it. My name was the first name at the top. There were four chairs at the table, but we didn't sit. We stood by the table and waited.

"Look at all of these people," said Marcus, he turned in a circle taking it all in.

Gavin leaned on the table almost making it tilt. His face was red.

"Nervous?" I asked.

"No!" he replied.

Charlotte tapped the table with her fingers and looked around. She smiled and waved to someone.

"Thank you, everyone!" Mrs. Russell's voice boomed over the loud speakers. "Thank you to parents for coming and supporting us today. Thank you to the teachers who have volunteered their time today. And thank you to students who came out to school on a Saturday to compete and learn a little more about STEM education. My hope is that we will have fun and learn in the process. As a reminder, parents to please stay behind the ropes so the teachers and other volunteers can come by and view the students as they work on the project."

Mrs. Russell went on to thank the teachers and parents from the other two schools, but I was trying not to pass out. I missed having gum to chew on. My tongue was getting sore. But then Mrs. Russell introduced a teacher from Holly Hills Elementary, and she was going to tell us the project we were to work on.

"Hi, everyone, my name is Mrs. Birchrum, and I teach third grade at Holly Hills Elementary." A cheer went up from a section in the gym. "I am glad to share what your project will be today. Today, you are going to create a catapult. Who among our students knows what a catapult is?" Mrs. Birchrum looked out at the students.

A red-haired girl raised her hand. "Yes? Penelope?" Mrs. Birchrum asked.

"It's something that can launch something further than we can throw it. It was used in the middle ages for attacking castles."

"Thank you, Penelope," Mrs. Birchrum replied. "Yes, you will make a catapult. Although not big enough to attack a castle. You are going to design a catapult to launch a ping-ping ball and a golf ball. They are both about the same size, but the golf ball weighs more than the ping pong ball. You will be measured on how far your catapult can throw both the ping pong ball and the golf ball. You will be given several Popsicle sticks, rubber bands, a plastic cup, and other small items to help you with your catapults. When the time is up, we have a line placed to measure how far you're able to launch the golf and ping pong balls. And don't forget that we will be looking for not only how far your catapult can go, but how well your group is working and planning together. We're going to see how creative you are with your idea as well. Remember we're looking at the whole process. But be

sure to have fun as well. Remember it's fun to make things. Good luck to everyone and have fun!"

Our table was handed a container with all of the items.

“Well, let’s begin,” I said.

Chapter 20 Building the Catapult

All four of us dove into the container.

"Look at all of these Popsicle sticks," said Marcus pulling them out and putting them on the table.

"I have the pencil and the planning sheet," said Charlotte pulling them out.

Gavin, of course, got the golf ball. "How far does this golf ball bounce?" Gavin took it and threw it hard on the gym floor, and he watched it bounce high into the air.

"Gavin! Don't bounce it. You'll lose it! And get us into trouble!" I shouted at him.

The ball landed back in his hand, "Okay! I have it." He smiled and waved it around showing off, and he put it back in the container. "And here is the ping pong ball!"

"Don't bounce it!" I shouted.

"I'm not going to bounce it," and he put it gently in the middle of the table.

The others looked at me and waited for me to give them instructions. "Okay, let's make sure we have everything we need. We already have the golf ball and the ping pong ball," I said.

"Looks like we have twenty Popsicle sticks," said Marcus.

"We also have a bag of rubber bands, and the cup to hold the ping pong and gold ball," said Charlotte as she pulled them out of the container.

"And a few paper clips, and a couple of binder clips," Marcus put them in the middle of the table, moving them away from his Popsicle stick pile.

"And two of these wooden dowel rods," said Charlotte.

"Okay, so anyone have an idea on how to build this thing by looking at all of these things?" said Gavin.

Charlotte held up one of the wooden rods, "We build the catapult around this. Watch. Hand me a stick."

Marcus handed her a Popsicle stick. She put the rod on the table and placed the stick across it. "Watch," she said. With her left index finger, she pushed the stick down to the table. With her right index finger, she pushed on the other end of the stick. The stick bent. Then she let her left index finger go, and the stick popped back up. It made a loud vibrating noise as it popped back into place.

"That works like a lever," said Marcus.

“Not like a lever, it is a lever,” I said. I took the planning paper and pencil from Charlotte. I drew a circle representing the rod and added a Popsicle stick to it. “See, we add the sticks to both sides of the binder clip, and from there we can add the cup onto one of the the sticks.”

Gavin looked in the container and pulled out the plastic cup. “These look like those sauce containers from Bob’s Chicken Sandwich Shop.”

“I like the barbecue sauce,” said Marcus taking the cup from Gavin.

“What do we do with the rubber bands?” asked Gavin, holding them up.

“We use those to hold the sticks in place, and I think we use the paper clips for the same reason,” I replied.

“Then we glue the cup onto one of the sticks,” said Gavin as he pulled the small bottle of glue out of the container and put it in the middle of the table.

“Yup,” I replied. “So, I think it should look like this.” And I added to the drawing. I labeled where the rubber bands, the paper clips, and the cup would go. I laid the paper in the middle of the table, as I saw an adult walk by with her clipboard. “What do you all think?” I said, hoping the adult with the clipboard didn’t think I was the only person in my group doing the planning. The adult stood behind Gavin, clicked her pen, and looked at us. My mouth went dry and couldn't speak for a moment. No one else spoke either.

Then Gavin rescued us.

"Okay! Hand me the rod and a couple sticks," he said. That helped us get going. I passed them to him, and Charlotte got a couple of rubber bands ready. We leaned into the table and began building, totally forgetting about the adult looking over us with the clipboard and pen.

A few minutes later, we had our first example of the catapult.

"Gavin, hand me the ping pong ball," I held my hand out to him and he gave me the ball. I put it in the cup. I pushed the catapult down and held it for a moment. Then I heard a snap and the ping-pong ball rolled away. The Popsicle stick had broken. "What! Oh no!" I exclaimed.

"Don't panic," said Charlotte. "We have time to fix it."

Marcus pulled another stick out of the pile. He sorted the sticks and handed me another one. "This must be why they gave us so many, extras for backups."

"But what about the cup? We glued it on!" Gavin worried. He picked up the broken half of the stick with the cup.

"Give it here," said Charlotte. And she gently twisted it and it came off. "The glue had not completely dried," she informed us, and she handed the cup back to me.

I took it from her, and I saw another adult standing behind Marcus, looking serious with a clipboard at the ready.

But this time we just kept working. We replaced the broken stick, then I glued the cup back on. In no time at all we had another catapult.

I handed it to Charlotte, "You give it a try. Maybe you won't break it."

She held down the stick with the cup and released it. The stick sprung back into place and made a loud vibrating sound.

"Whew!" I wiped my forehead. "Let's try it with the ping pong ball." I handed Charlotte the ball.

She put it in the cup and tried the catapult one more time. The ball flew out of the cup and over the table.

"Cool!" shouted Marcus.

"Yes!" Gavin grinned as he chased the ping pong ball across the floor.

"Excuse me," one of the teachers stood by the stage and tapped the microphone once more, "but I just wanted to let everyone know we have five minutes before we test our catapults, just wanted to let you be aware of the time."

"Let's test it with the golf ball to make sure it doesn't break, and if it does, we hopefully can fix it if needed," I said to the rest of the group.

"Good idea," replied Charlotte.

Gavin took the golf ball out of the container and rolled it across the table to me. I slid the ball and the catapult to Charlotte. "You try. I trust your touch," I told her.

"Let's stand behind her," said Marcus. "I don't feel like getting hit in the head with a golf ball."

"Good idea," agreed Gavin.

They scooted over to our side of the table and stood behind Charlotte. Charlotte pushed down gently on the catapult arm and let it go. The arm flung the golf ball into the air and it arched over the table. The ball bounced about five feet past our table and started to roll.

"I got it!" Gavin exclaimed and he bolted around the table. The ball rolled under the rope into the walkway. Gavin slid under the rope like a baseball player. His foot kicked the ball and it took off underneath another rope and towards other tables with students from the other schools. And Gavin just kept going after it.

It bounced past a teacher with a clipboard, and Gavin ignored the teacher and just kept going.

"Be careful!" the teacher exclaimed.

It rolled under Juan and Kadan's table. They were busy on their own catapults and as the ball bounced by their feet.

"Hey!" Juan shouted as Gavin reached between his legs for the golf ball. Juan crashed onto Gavin. Gavin stood up and picked Juan up as he did.

"Sorry about that!" Gavin brushed Juan off, he ran around their table picked the ball up. He jogged back to us, apologizing to Juan and their table as he came back.

"I'm sorry about that," he kept his head down as he approached our table.

I pointed at him, "You are lucky you didn't knock their table over! And oh-my-goodness I hope that little disaster didn't hurt us in being graded. Ugh!" I almost pulled my hair out.

Charlotte patted me on the back, "But he didn't knock anything or anyone over. It's time to measure how far our catapult can throw." She pointed to the stage where Mrs. Birchrum was walking to the microphone.

She tapped the microphone, "Excuse me, ladies

and gentlemen. Excuse me. Please step away from your work. It is time to finally measure your work. I am excited! I hope you are too! We are going to come around and escort you to where we will measure your catapult."

Marcus clapped and rubbed his hands together, "Yeah! Let's do this!"

I took a deep breath, "I think we're ready."

Chapter 21 The Gym

We stood behind a long line of blue tape. There were labels for where each team was to line up. Past the blue line, there were several yellow lines that stretched across the gym. To the left the lines connected with another yellow line that ran perpendicular. That line was labeled with marks for inches and feet.

It stretched out ten feet. I couldn't believe that the teachers think we could launch a ball that far, ten feet, with these catapults.

"So, I guess we're aiming for the ten-foot line," said Gavin pointing to the farthest yellow line.

"I guess we are," I replied.

"Yeah we are!" Marcus rubbed his hands together and nodded his head.

"Shh!" Charlotte shushed us and pointed to Mrs. Birchrum.

Mrs. Birchrum stood passed the last yellow line holding a microphone. "Thank you everyone for quickly getting into place and following the adult volunteers. As you can see in front of me there are some yellow lines. This will help us measure how far each ping-pong and golf ball will go. For this part of the competition we will have three launches of the ping pong ball. We will record your farthest launch. Next, we will we repeat with the golf ball. We will have three launches of the golf ball, and we will again record your farthest launch with the golf ball. We will add the total distance of your best ping pong launch with your best golf ball launch. There will be an adult volunteer or teacher with each team to help measure your throw."

I looked behind us and saw a teacher step in behind us. She smiled, waved at me, and then pointed back at Mrs. Birchrum.

"When we give the instruction to launch, please stay behind the blue line. Volunteers will retrieve and return the ball to you. The ping pong and golf balls will be labeled with your team number, making it easy to measure and return the ball. So, at this time the adult with you will give you your ping pong ball and help you get ready."

The teacher behind us handed me a yellow ping pong ball with the number two written on it. "Hi guys, I'm Mrs. Jackson. I'm just here to see if you need any help and to measure how far the ball goes." She waved a clipboard.

"Hi, Mrs. Jackson," replied Charlotte and we all introduced ourselves.

"Thanks, I don't think we need any help," I took the ball and placed it in the catapult and set the catapult. I held my finger on it.

"Okay, let's do this thing!" Gavin said into my ear.

"Be quiet," I told him.

Mrs. Birchrum spoke, "Okay teams, if we're ready on the count of three, let's do our first launch." She held her right hand in the air, "Three, two, and one!" She dropped her right hand.

I let my finger go, and the ball launched into the air. Everyone in the gym cheered as the ping-pong balls launched into the air. I watched our yellow ball arch into the air and land squarely on the five-foot line.

"Five feet!" exclaimed Mrs. Jackson and she recorded the number on her clipboard. "Just a second Gavin, I'll go and get the ball."

Gavin looked disappointed to not chase the ball across the gym. People laughed as teachers chased the ten ping pong balls across the gym.

Charlotte pointed to the far end of the gym, "That team looks like their ball landed around the nine-foot line."

I realized I didn't even see how any other team had done. I was just pleased ours made it five feet. "Whose team is that?" I asked.

Marcus walked back and looked down the gym, "Shoot! I think it's Juan's team!"

"Ugh! Of course it's his team," I said.

Mrs. Jackson brought the ball back, and Mrs. Birchrum congratulated all of us on a great first throw.

"And it seems Team Nine had a really good launch with a nine-foot launch," she smiled and pointed at the team.

"Marcus, you do the second launch," I instructed, and I got out of the way.

Marcus nodded his head and bounced to the catapult. "Oh yeah, let's get this done." He said as he squatted down to put his finger on the catapult.

I whispered to Charlotte, "Keep an eye on how far Juan's team launches their ball."

Mrs. Birchrum counted down from three and Marcus let the ball fly.

"There she goes!" he shouted.

The ball looked to land a couple of inches short of the six-foot line.

"That looks like six feet to me," said Mrs. Jackson. I almost said something, but then kept my mouth shut.

"How did Juan do?" I asked Charlotte.

"It looked like seven feet," she replied.

"It looks like Team Six did very well this round with a launch of eight feet," announced Mrs. Birchrum.

People clapped and cheered.

I looked down the line. "That's a fifth-grade team," I told the rest of my team. I clapped my hands, "But it doesn't matter which team it is. We just need to do our best. Gavin, give it a try."

Gavin pumped both fists in the air. "Bring on the Ping Pong!"

"That's funny," Charlotte said.

"It is," agreed Marcus, "Why didn't I think of it."

"Do your thing Gavin," I said, secretly praying that he wouldn't break it.

Mrs. Birchrum raised her hand and counted down and the ping pong balls launched. Our yellow ping pong took off like a rocket, and then seemed to hold in space as it reached the top of its arc. And it came back down to earth and bounced squarely on the eight-foot line.

"Eight feet!" Gavin lifted both fists in the air.

"Nicely done, Gavin!" said Mrs. Jackson.

"If I am correct it looks like Team Two may have been our winner for that round with a launch of eight feet," said Mrs. Birchrum. The gym erupted into applause.

"Why is everyone clapping for us? Juan beat us

with the nine-foot launch earlier?" asked Gavin.

"You did well, and they are cheering you on Gavin," Mrs. Jackson encouraged him. "And looking at your scores of five, six, and eight feet you are doing very well. I don't know what the other teams have, but no matter what, you all have built a strong catapult." She handed me a golf ball, and like the ping pong it was yellow with a two on it.

I handed the ball to Charlotte, "You haven't gone yet, and your launch is what sent Gavin chasing it across the room. Let's see if you have that same luck this time."

"Okay, as I mentioned before, this is the golf ball portion of our event. Your best golf ball launch will be combined with your best ping-pong launch. Again, please remain behind the blue line and let the adults retrieve the balls. Everyone should now have their golf ball, and if you are ready let's begin the count down." She raised her hand again and counted down. "Three! Two! One!"

Charlotte let the ball go and it made a beautiful arc, and it landed on the seven-and a half foot line.

"Seven feet and six inches! Impressive ladies and gentlemen!" Mrs. Jackson cheered us on.

Mrs. Jackson ran out and came back from retrieving the ball. Mrs. Birchrum came over the speakers. "It looks like Team Two out launched everyone with that one. I think it was seven feet six inches. Correct?"

"That's correct," Mrs. Jackson replied to her.

"Let Charlotte shoot it again," said Gavin.

Marcus nodded his head, "I agree. She did well with it."

They were right, no need to mess with something that is working, "Yeah, I agree. Charlotte, you do the next one as well."

She just shrugged her shoulders, "Okay." She crouched down and the got catapult ready for the next shot. She gently pulled the catapult down with her right hand. With her left hand she grasped the front part of the catapult. No one else in our group had done that.

Mrs. Birchrum counted down again, "Three, two, one!"

Charlotte let the catapult launch. The ball took off and did a nice smooth arc. It hit the seven-foot line and bounced further on.

"Seven feet!" said Mrs. Jackson.

"Nice!" Marcus pumped his fist.

"Good job!" Gavin clapped.

"Nicely done, Charlotte!" I said. "Who won that round?"

"Congratulations to Team Nine with a launch of seven feet six inches," Mrs. Birchrum announced.

"Juan's team," we all moaned at the same time.

"And by just a few inches," replied Charlotte.

"Well, you'll get them this time," I said.

"This is the last throw. Shouldn't you or someone else do it?" Charlotte replied.

"You should do it. The way you hold the catapult seems to be working," I said. "Plus, with this being the last launch, I don't want to learn how to launch the golf ball. You're doing a good job. Let's keep going."

"I agree with Sally," Gavin said. "It's the last throw and you've done a good job with it."

"Thanks guys," Charlotte smiled.

"Here you go," said Mrs. Jackson handing her the golf ball.

Charlotte took the ball placed it on the catapult, crawled down onto the floor. She squinted with one eye. She held the catapult with her left hand and held the catapult's arm down with her right.

Mrs. Birchrum spoke louder into the microphone,

"Okay, ladies and gentlemen. This is it, our last launch, so good luck. And remember, we will take your best throw of the golf ball and the ping pong ball. Your total score is not only these launches, but how you did working as a group. So, don't panic, relax, do your best, and have fun." She raised her hand, "So, count down with me. Three, two, one!"

Charlotte let the ball go and it shot off like a rocket. It seemed to hover in the air for a little bit and then it came down with a smack! Right on the eight-foot line! That's my girl! I didn't see the other teams, but I sensed she got it.

Mrs. Birchrum spoke into her microphone, "It looks like Team 2, got that round with an eight-foot launch. Am I correct Mrs. Jackson?"

Mrs. Jackson put her thumb in the air, "Yes! Hit the eight-foot line."

"Well, congrats to Team Two for that. But now is the time where we will take a moment, tally the launches of all the catapults, and we will come back with the results of our competition!"

"Ugh! We have to wait," moaned Gavin.

"It will only be a few minutes," replied Mrs. Jackson.

"Hey guys! You guys did amazing!" said a voice behind us. I turned and looked, and it was Aaron. He was wearing his baseball uniform. It was covered in dirt.

"Hey dude! You came!" shouted Marcus and he ran over to him.

"Thanks for coming," I said.

"Yeah, sorry I missed it. But we won our game and it sent us into the playoffs," he smiled.

"Well, that's awesome," I replied.

"Cool!" Marcus gave him a high five.

Mrs. Jackson patted me on the back, "You guys did a great job. But it looks like we're about to get the results back," she pointed to Mrs. Birchrum coming back to the microphone.

She was ready with the results.

Chapter 22 The Results

She tapped the microphone, "Okay, everyone, we're ready to share the results."

We all turned face her, and the gym was suddenly quiet.

"Thanks again for giving me your attention so quickly," Mrs. Birchrum said into the microphone.

"That's because we want to know the results," Gavin complained under his breath.

I shushed him.

Mrs. Birchrum continued, "Just a reminder, we determined our winners based on how far the catapult threw the ball and how well you worked together and planned. And now having said that, I want to say how much we all enjoyed going around and watching you work together creating, planning, and using your catapults." She looked at a piece of paper, "Here are the results. In third place, from Holly Hills, Team Four."

Team Four screamed and jumped up and down. We clapped politely. The people around the gym clapped. "Well, come and get your ribbons Team Four." The team walked out to Mrs. Birchrum and got their ribbons. My stomach went into knots.

"Congratulations again to Team Four. And in second place, from Cedarwood Road Elementary, Team

Five." Team Five jumped and screamed. Parents from Cedarwood Road cheered and clapped. Team Five ran out, picked up their ribbons, and ran back to their spot waving their ribbons.

"That was a little weird," said Marcus looking at me.

I shrugged, "They were excited."

"Act like you belong here," said Gavin.

"What do you mean?" Charlotte asked.

"Don't act like that," he pointed to Team Five. "Act like you knew you were going to win."

"They were rightfully excited Gavin," Charlotte replied to him.

"Okay guys, quiet, here it comes," I told them. My heart felt like it was going to jump out of my chest.

Mrs. Birchum cleared her throat. And she showed four trophies next to her. And she motioned to them, "Okay, and in first place, from Turing Elementary, is Team Two."

Gavin jumped twelve feet into the air and then ran out to get his trophy from Mrs. Birchrum.

"So much for acting like you belong here," said Charlotte smiling as she followed Gavin out to Mrs. Birchrum.

Marcus grinned as he headed out to get his trophy.

My head felt fuzzy. And then I realized what had happened, we won.

I followed the rest of my team out to the middle of the gym to get our trophies.

Mrs. Birchrum handed me the trophy. I felt a grin stretch across my face. I couldn't hold it in.

"And here you go, Sally," Mrs. Birchrum handed me a trophy. "Congratulations on your and your team's great work! Team Two is from here at Turing Elementary School. Who is your teacher?"

"Mrs. King," I replied into the microphone. I heard people several people cheer louder. My parents and brothers were jumping up and down. I could see Jackson jumping up and down with his cast bouncing in between Mom and Dad.

Charlotte jumped on my back and I nearly fell over. Gavin and Marcus joined her in jumping on me. "Okay! Okay! You all are going to break me."

Mrs. Birchrum spoke once more into the microphone, "Thank you parents for bringing your child out on a Saturday. You can find your child and then please check in with their teacher before you leave. And thank you to the teachers and our volunteers for coming to help today. Thank you again everyone for coming out to our STEM competition. We hope to see everyone here again next year."

My parents came out from behind the rope to come and get me. Mom hugged me tight and Dad gave me a high-five. Jackson jammed his cast into my back as he hugged me.

"Congrats! Buddy!" Michael patted me on the head.

"Sally, I am so proud of you all!" Mrs. Russell came up behind me and hugged me from the side. "I knew you all would do well! Congratulations!"

I saw Juan come over. He gave me a high-five, "Nicely done!" he said.

"Why didn't you all win?" I asked. "I think your first throw of the ping pong ball would have made you the longest launches and therefore the winner of that part."

Juan shrugged his shoulders, "Ah, we had someone on our team not really be a team player and I think that cost us. They saw us arguing a lot and one person just sitting down on the side at one moment. So, that wasn't great I admit."

"Well, I was very impressed with your catapult."

"Maybe next year we can work together on a team," said Juan.

"We'll see," I replied, knowing I would keep my

Number Investigators together.

"I say we have a meeting tonight," suggested Charlotte.

"I agree," I replied.

Chapter 23 The Treehouse Meeting

"Here Ye! Here Ye!" Charlotte pounded the gavel on the floor of her treehouse later. We all had our STEM trophies sitting next to us. "I call this meeting of The Number Investigators to order." She kept pounding the floor of the treehouse.

We all covered our ears. We were all there, Charlotte, me, Marcus, Aaron, and now Gavin.

"Give me that!" and Marcus took the gavel.

"What is on your agenda tonight?" Gavin asked.

"I don't have one. Sally, do you have one?"

"I do have an idea." I reached into my backpack and pulled out the catapult, a ping pong ball, and a golf ball.

"Now that's what I am talking about," Marcus got excited and rubbed his hands together.

"Cool, I didn't to get try it," said Aaron.

"Well, we have time now," I said and put a ping pong ball in and launched it across the treehouse.

About the author

Martin Tiller is an elementary school teacher in Richmond, Virginia.

He is also the author of The Dolbin School series, The Kevin Books Series, and The Number Invesigators. He can be found at martintillerauthor.com and Martin Tiller Author on Facebook.

Stop by and say hello.

Made in United States
North Haven, CT
15 March 2023

34101348R00075